C000126895

Finn Feels Be

Written by Jessica Ellis

Illustrated by Parwinder Singh

Collins

Finn feels sad.

He and Mum go to his room.

Finn looks in the box.

He sees his things.

Finn can see his light.

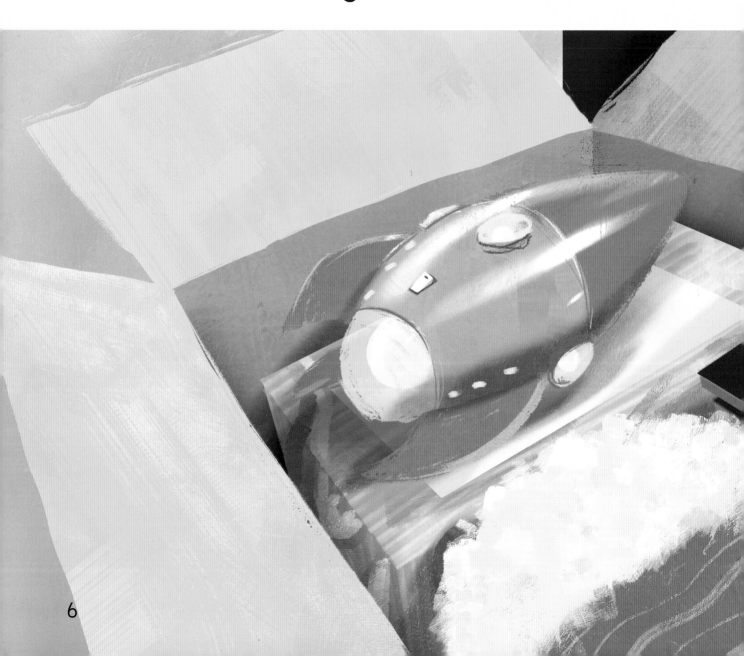

He can see his art.

Finn sees his letters.

He sees his cool towel.

Finn sees his coat.

He hangs it on his hook.

Finn turns to Mum.

12

Finn feels better

 Review: After reading

Use your assessment from hearing the children read to choose any GPCs, words or tricky words that need additional practice.

Read 1: Decoding

- Ask the children to look through the book and find words with the /ee/ sound in them. (*feels/feel, sees/see*)
- Can they think of any words that rhyme with **hook**? (e.g. *book, look, took, crook, brook*)

Read 2: Prosody

- Model reading each page with expression to the children. After you have read each page, ask the children to have a go at reading with expression.
- On page 13 discuss how Finn would say the phrase in the speech bubble.

Read 3: Comprehension

- Look at pages 14 to 15. Discuss the sequence of the story and what happened to make Finn feel better.
- For every question ask the children how they know the answer. Ask:
  - Why do you think Finn is feeling sad at the beginning of the story? (*he has just moved house and it feels a bit strange/different*)
  - Why are all of Finn's belongings in a box? (*they were packed to move house and he hasn't unpacked yet*)
  - What items does Finn find in the box? (*his light, his art, his letters, his cool towel and his coat*)
  - What special things would you pack if you were moving house?
  - Why do you think Finn feels better on page 13? (*because he has all his things back and it feels like home now*)